DREAM MACHINES

by

MARK ROGALSKI

RP|KIDS
PHILADELPHIA · LONDON

9 8 7 6 5 4 3 2 1
Digit on the right indicates the number of this printing

Library of Congress Control Number: 2008920180

ISBN 978-0-7624-3261-5

Cover and interior design by Mark Rogalski & Ryan Hayes
Edited by Jon Anderson and T.L. Bonaddio
Typography: Adobe Garamond Pro, Futura, Lucida Sans, Rockwell

Published by Running Press Kids, an imprint of
Running Press Book Publishers
2300 Chestnut Street
Philadelphia, PA 19103-4371

Visit us on the web!
www.runningpress.com

For Madison & Sarah

For Jack - my best friend,
with lots of love.
                    Doru
                    08 April, 2010

Bed time! Bath time!
Hello, moon!
Night has come,
But it's too soon!

You wish you may,
You wish you might.
You wish to play
All through the night.

But wishes need
A wishing star.
Lacking that
You won't get far.

Can you find one?
Do you dare?
Just one path
Will take you there.

Along the way
Are Dream Machines,
To help you move
Between the scenes.

Not just a game,
This wish will start
A quest for what's
Within your heart.

So stay awake
By any means,
And climb aboard
The Dream Machines.

THE
BUBBLE SUB

Into the tub!
It's time to begin.
Dream up a sub
To take for a spin.

Fill up the bath.
Then fill it more!
Your Bubble Sub
Is built to explore!

Find a Sea Wee.
Where can they be?
If you are lucky
Move ahead three.

timely tip

timely tip

You're doing well
When you advance.
On your next move
Beware of plants.

THE
SEA WEE COLLECTION

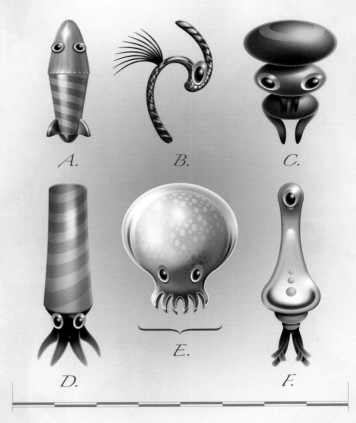

A.   B.   C.

D.   E.   F.

A is for Abner, look under your rug.

B is for Basil, more ugh than a bug.

C is for Collette, her mother's an eel.

D is for Desmond, who makes a good meal.

E is for Everett, he knows how to knit.

F is for Fanny, who just likes to sit.

THE
DRAGONFLIER

Yes, your tub did overflow.
And things have now begun to grow.
Creatures that you do not know
Are filling up the house. Oh no!

Before the fish get too gung ho,
And crocodiles can say hello,
You must escape the murky flow
To find your star, this much you know.

A Dragonflier can hover low
Above the danger just below.
It's yours to use, yet even so,
You lose one turn before you go.

 · · ·

DID YOU KNOW...

DID YOU KNOW...

You're heading out
To deeper water.
Are you certain
That you ought'er?

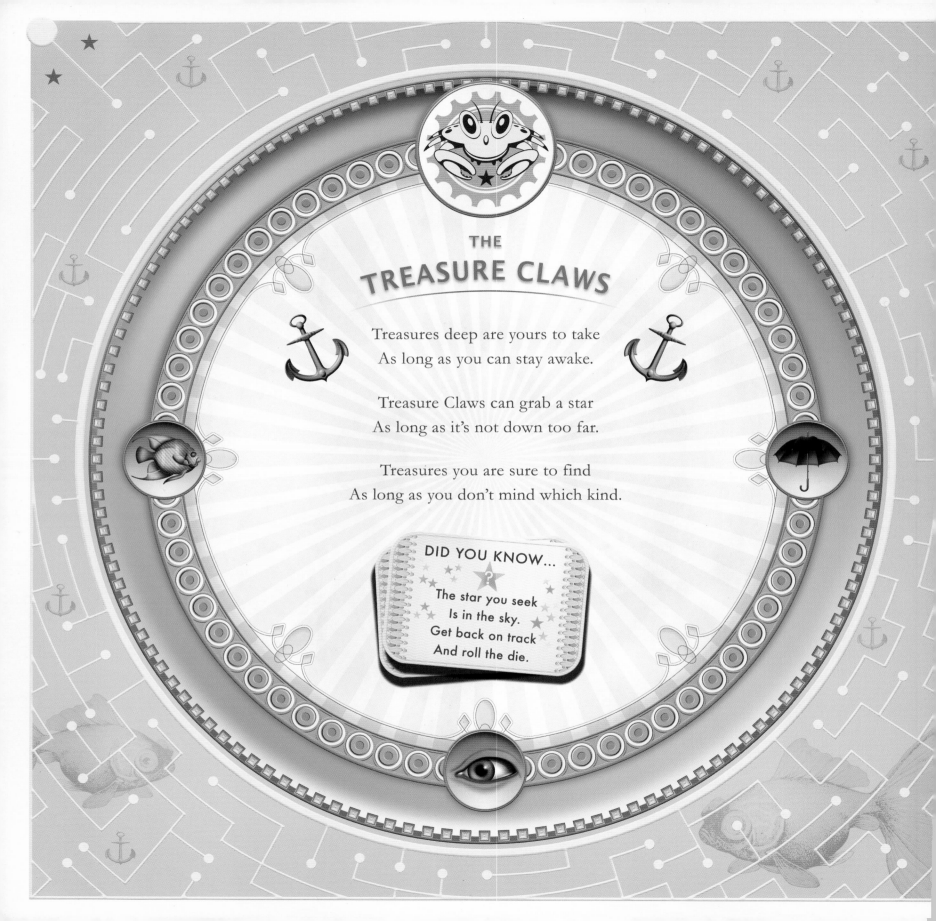

THE
TREASURE CLAWS

Treasures deep are yours to take
As long as you can stay awake.

Treasure Claws can grab a star
As long as it's not down too far.

Treasures you are sure to find
As long as you don't mind which kind.

DID YOU KNOW...

The star you seek
Is in the sky.
Get back on track
And roll the die.

THE
OCTOPOD

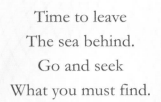

Time to leave
The sea behind.
Go and seek
What you must find.

On dry land
Pursue your wish.
Just beware
Of flying fish!

Pedal fast
To win your race.
Move ahead
Another space.

CRAZY CARD

I spy with my eye
Something fishy in the sky.

Lose 1 turn.

CRAZY CARD

North is up, South is not.
East and West, you forgot.

Spin back 4 spaces.

CRAZY CARD

Little ant. Monkey's uncle.
Elephant has a trunkful.

Go back 3 spaces.

CRAZY CARD

Octopi cannot fly
Even though they try and try.

Pedal back 6 spaces.

timely tip

To reach your star
Is extra hard
If you draw a
Crazy Card.

THE
BALL BEARING

Can you bear
To find a star
With no guide
Who travels far?

This bear moves
Just round and round.
He won't go
Where stars are found.

Roll your dice.
Spin your spinner.
Free yourself
To be a winner!

timely tip

You will not fail
If you stay
On the trail.

THE
SNOW MOBILE

Oh, dear, your trail
Has gotten cold.
But also hot.
Where have you rolled?

Hot on the trail?
Your star in sight?
Or frozen stiff?
Call it a night?

When cool is hot
And hot is cool,
The Snow Mobile
Is just the tool!

HOT SPOT

You're Puddle Jump Champ
Once again!
Take a leap, hop up 10.

HOT SPOT

Spaceship lands
At your door!
Aliens transport you 4.

HOT SPOT

Squirting Flower
Magic Tricks!
Hocus-pocus move up 6.

timely tip

Hot Spots chase
The chills away.
You can't win
If you can't play.

HOT SPOT

My, you like the
Squid Pie Stew!
Don't stop at 1, please take 2.

THE
WIND GARDENS

You've tested deep waters.
You've roamed 'cross the land.
The sky is now calling,
And, boy, is it grand!

Good sailors know wind.
Skilled pilots, the sky.
Wind Gardeners, you ask?
They plant, grow, and fly.

So pull up those roots!
Let the launching begin!
Your star's getting closer.
You might even win!

DID YOU KNOW...
❋ ❋ ❋
With the right seed
You will succeed!
What you grow
Is where you'll go.

ROCKET NOVELTY
SEEDS
PROPELLOR
PEAS

ROCKET NOVELTY
SEEDS
ORANGE
BREEZE

ROCKET NOVELTY
SEEDS
FLYING
ONIONS
FROM
BELIZE

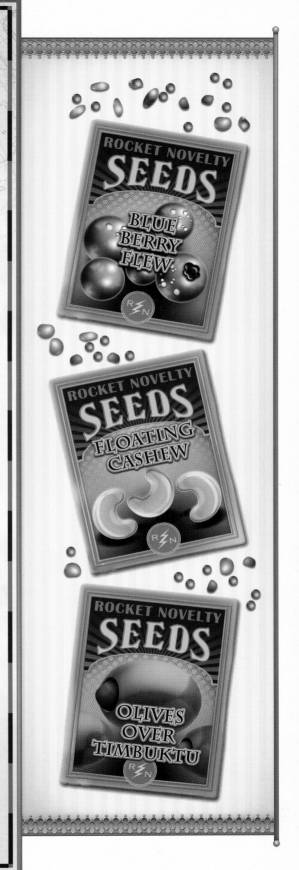

ROCKET NOVELTY
SEEDS
BLUE
BERRY
FLEW

ROCKET NOVELTY
SEEDS
FLOATING
CASHEW

ROCKET NOVELTY
SEEDS
OLIVES
OVER
TIMBUKTU

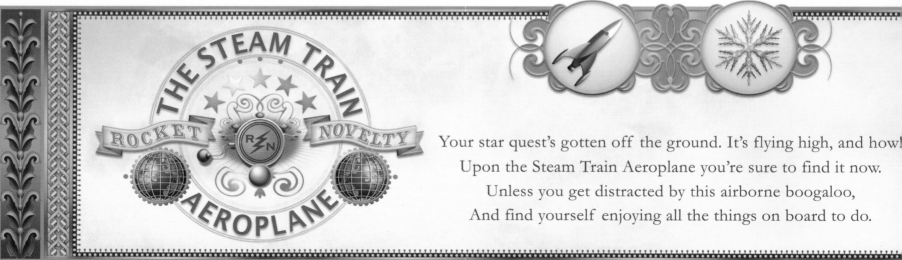

THE STEAM TRAIN AEROPLANE
ROCKET · R/N · NOVELTY

Your star quest's gotten off the ground. It's flying high, and how!
Upon the Steam Train Aeroplane you're sure to find it now.
Unless you get distracted by this airborne boogaloo,
And find yourself enjoying all the things on board to do.

Bedtime stories, laboratories, lots of pings and pongs.
Late night snacks with piggybacks and slumber party songs.
Pack your bags and jump on board, it's all full steam ahead.
Fly around the world tonight before you go to bed!

DID YOU KNOW...
A flying train
That has no drain
Can't take fish
To the moon.

DID YOU KNOW...
To make that trip,
You'll need a ship
Part water-filled
Balloon.

THE
WATER BALLOONS

A Three of Sharks,
A Two of Squids,
Have joined the Ace of Whales,
To share a proper spot of tea,
And aquanautic tales.

Ride with them
To the thermosphere
Where air turns into space.
When you're done, say "Pardon me!"
And go on with your race.

GLOBO del AGUA

A PROPER TIN OF TEA

NOVEL TEA

TOO HOT · TO HOOT

FROM ROCKET NOVELTY

DID YOU KNOW...

Some tea, you see,
Can be the key
To help your kelp
Keep worry-free.

You've reached the moon!
—At least some version—
Adrift amidst
Your space excursion.

Hear its music!
Hear its strings!
Hear the lullaby it sings!

"Close your eyes,"
It calls to you.
"If you don't dream,
Dreams can't come true."

But shake it off,
You're almost there.
You can win it, fair and square.

DID YOU KNOW...

To fall asleep
By the light of the moon
Would end your game
A bit too soon.

THE
WISHING STAR

You've found the final Dream Machine,
And, yes, it's quite a sight.
But on the way you may have lost
The meaning of your flight.

It's not about the star at all,
But the journey that you took.
For joy is in the things you see
Not those you overlook.

You wished to play and that you did,
And, yes you won the game.
Just stay awake a moment more,
There's one card left to claim.